# To town

by Joy Cowley

I will go to town
on my bulldozer,
my big yellow bulldozer.

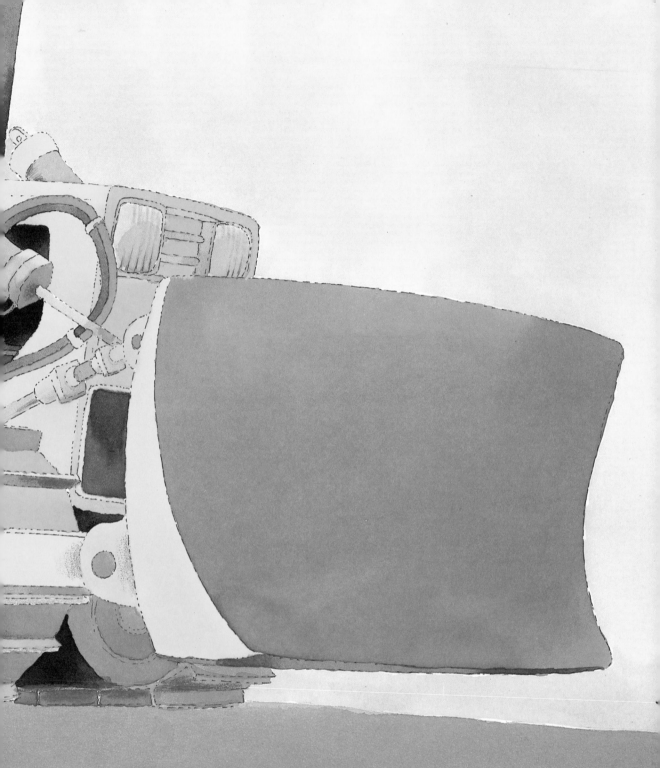

Brr-rrr, brr-rrr,
all the way to town.

I will go to town
in my fire engine,
my big red fire engine.

4

Ooooo – aaaah – ooooo – aaaah,

all the way to town.

I will go to town
in my vintage car,
my big green vintage car.

Toot-a-toot, toot-a-toot,
all the way to town.

I will go to town
in my helicopter,
my big blue helicopter.

Choppa-choppa,
choppa-choppa,
all the way to town.

I will go to town
on my motor bike,
my big orange motor bike.

**Brrrrm, brrrrm,
all the way to town.**

I will go to town
on my pogo stick,
my super silver
pogo stick.

Boing, boing,
boing, boing,
all the way to town.

All the way to town,

14

and then...

Boing Boing Boing Boing

all the way
back home again.